Charlotte in Paris

BY JOAN MACPHAIL KNIGHT

ILLUSTRATIONS BY MELISSA SWEET

GIVERNY
PARIS

Giverny

Monsieur et
Madame
Glidden

April 28, 1893
Rue de l'Amiscourt
Giverny

The postman has been very grumpy lately. He says there are so many American painters here in Giverny that he can scarcely lift his mailbag with all the letters he has to carry. He handed me an important-looking letter addressed to Monsieur et Madame Glidden.

When Papa came home from painting at the river, he let me open the envelope. It's an invitation to Paris! A Miss Mary Cassatt is having an exhibition. Papa says she is the most famous woman painter in all of Europe. The Fosters will be going, too. Lizzy Foster is my best friend. When Papa decided to come to Giverny a year ago, Lizzy and I missed each other so much. Then Mr. Foster decided he also wanted to learn the new French way of painting called Impressionism. So the Fosters have come to Giverny and rented a house right down the street from us.

Last night, we had our neighbors the Perrys to dinner to meet the Fosters. Edith Perry is my age and she has a little dog named Degas just like my dog, Toby. Raymonde set the table out in the garden and cooked a special dinner of tiny roast hens with their feet tied together. For dessert, we had "Tarte Tatin," a delicious upside-down apple cake.

Edith and I told Lizzy all about our famous neighbor, Monsieur Monet. When we got to the part about the water garden and the Japanese bridge, Lizzy had to see for herself. We climbed the garden wall and crept along the mossy stones past Monsieur Monet's hothouse to the bamboo forest until we could see the Japanese bridge...and Monsieur Monet could see us! We had such a fright, we fell to the ground. I hope Mama never finds out about this. She always tells me to mind my own affairs.

May 20, 1893
Rue de l'Amiscourt
Giverny

This morning I sat in a green field and painted a picture of bright red poppies.
Then I saw something I have never seen before: fifteen or twenty ladies riding
bicycles right down the middle of the road. Toby ran after them, barking, and
disappeared in the cloud of dust the bicycles made. I was glad when he came
running back to me—a dusty little ball of fur!

les coquelicots

Mama says the young ladies are from America, here to learn about painting "en plein air"—outdoors— instead of in a studio. But she thinks they are more interested in young men and lawn tennis than they are in art classes.

Not like Miss Emmet, who was having tea with Mama when I got home. She asked Raymonde if she would sit for a portrait. "Pourquoi pas?" said Raymonde. Why not? Miss Emmet wanted her to wear her apron but Raymonde said no. She wants her portrait painted in her Sunday best, just like everybody else.

la ficelle

trois bâtons

les pois de senteur

Later, Lizzy came by with some sweet pea seeds she brought from Appledore Island back home. We planted them along the sunny wall behind my garden. Then we found just the right spot for the pumpkin seeds that Monsieur Seurel gave me. He is the best gardener in the world and knows everything there is to know about a vegetable garden, or "potager" as he calls it. On the seed packet it says "Rouge vif d'Etampes." I have never heard of bright red pumpkins before. I can't wait to see them!

When I looked out my window this morning, I counted twenty-two workmen digging in Monsieur Monet's garden! Monsieur Seurel says the water garden is taking more time and money to build than Monsieur Monet thought it would. The cowherds say his new plants are poisoning the water. Monsieur Seurel thinks cowherds should concern themselves with cows, not the affairs of "le grand maître," the great master.

      Mrs. Perry says Monsieur Monet is the finest landscape painter in the world. No one can paint water and the way light falls on it the way he can. Is that what the water garden is for, I wonder? For painting? Or is it to put pike fish on the table as Monsieur Seurel thinks?

The Japanese Bridge in
Monsieur Monet's Garden

le brochet

le saule
pleureur

un petit pont

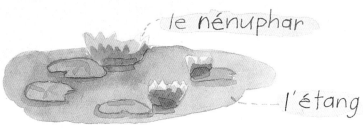

le nénuphar

l'étang

My tutor, Mademoiselle Bertout, came today. She said I spend so much time looking out the window at the water garden, I should learn the French words for what I see there.

As soon as the lesson was over, I ran to Lizzy's. They're packing to go to the seacoast. Lucky Lizzy! I wish we could go along, but Papa says there is far too much to do here in Giverny. "Tant pis!" Too bad! Lizzy promised to bring me back a bucketful of seashells.

 le chevalet

 la boîte de couleurs

L'AUTOPORTRAIT

 la palette

 le pinceau

Monsieur Monet rushed past me this morning, his arms filled with paints and canvases. If I hadn't jumped aside, he would have bumped into me. I ran to find Mrs. Perry. Surely, she would know where he was off to in such a hurry.

Through the studio window, I could see her painting a portrait of herself. She looked very serious. I waited until she put her paintbrush down to speak, just as Papa taught me.

"Maybe he went to Rouen," she said. "He spoke about painting the cathedral there. Of course, I haven't seen much of him lately," she went on, "he is in such a black mood."

At first, I was afraid Monsieur Monet had told her about the other night. But then she went on to say that all the American painters are driving him away. They want painting lessons and Monsieur Monet doesn't believe painting can be taught. He says painters have to discover things on their own.

Tonight we went to the Baudy Hotel for supper. It was as noisy as ever, with everyone talking and laughing at once. Madame Baudy brought over a saucer of milk for Toby and a "petit bifteck," a tiny steak. I had to shout to tell her we are going to Paris for the exhibition. She said Mademoiselle Cassatt has been a guest at the hotel on more than one occasion. Not only that, she has a dog just like Toby. Its name is Batty and she takes it everywhere. Just like me!

July 1, 1893
Rue de l'Amiscourt
Giverny

Today Mama had Miss Hale to tea in the garden. She just got back from painting school in Paris. Mama wanted to know all about what the ladies there are wearing. "Ostrich feathers and silks," said Miss Hale. The only feathers here are chicken feathers! Mama will have to wait until we get to Paris if she wants feathers of another kind.

Later, I went to the kitchen to see what Raymonde was doing. She was sitting at the table with the postman. He stops in after his rounds for a glass of wine and some talk. Today he brought a card from Lizzy!

EPPE. — Le Bain.

On the back it says: Hotel des Roches Noires, Trouville

Our hotel is called "Hotel of the Black Rocks." That's because the rocks
are covered with seaweed. There are more painters here than boats on the sea.
One of them is Monsieur Monet! Today he had a temper tantrum and threw his
paintbox into the waves. I learned how to dive. A bientôt! See you soon!

Love, Lizzy

When I read the card out loud the postman laughed. He said it won't
be the first time Monsieur Monet has to telegraph Paris for a new paintbox.
And then he remarked that artists aren't like other people. Why, just today
he saw something "très curieux," very unusual, in the garden of Monsieur et
Madame MacMonnies. Who are the MacMonnies, I wonder? And what did
the postman see?

les coquilles

une étoile de mer

une moule

une huître

A painting I made
using tiny dots of color.

Charlotte

July 2, 1893
In Papa's studio
Giverny

Papa is very busy. He wants to finish twenty-five canvases before we go to Paris. Monsieur Durand-Ruel, the gallery owner there, says he can sell them all. Not only that, Monsieur Durand-Ruel found an apartment for us to stay in when we visit Paris. It has a large studio next to it, for Papa and Mr. Foster to share. Mama says we'll be there for six months. We're even going to bring Raymonde. I'm glad because I'd miss her if we didn't. But Mademoiselle Bertout will stay here in Giverny. "Paris is an education itself," says Papa. I'm happy about that. "Plus de leçons!" No more lessons!

Now Papa is finishing a portrait he started of Mr. Foster in the garden. He is trying a new way of painting, called pointillism. It takes a very long time to do. He has to cover the canvas with tiny dots of color. When I stand close to it the dots make me dizzy and I can't tell what it's about. But when I look at it from the other side of the studio everything falls into place. I like his old way of painting better. I wondered if Papa would sell this one. But he says it is just an exercise and not for sale. He tells me it's important for an artist to try new ways of seeing things.

la citronnade

July 12, 1893
Rue de l'Amiscourt
Giverny

Lizzy is back and this morning we found out what the postman saw! Mrs. Suzanne Butler, Monsieur Monet's daughter, was pushing her pram along the Chemin du Roy. We ran after her to see her new baby. All at once, she turned the corner and disappeared through a garden gate. The gate was too tall to see over so we unlatched it and followed her in.

la voiture
d'enfant

le bébé

le chapeau
de soleil

    Mrs. Butler's baby smiled at us. Over by the stream we saw a woman wearing no clothes at all—not even her bloomers! She was having her portrait painted in the sun.

    Mrs. Butler introduced us to the artist, Mrs. MacMonnies, who invited us all into her studio for cakes and lemonade. The model put on a robe and came along, too. Her name is Lisette and she is from Paris. Mrs. MacMonnies has hired her to pose for the whole summer. No wonder Mrs. MacMonnies paints in her own garden!

mes bottines

mes chaussures
de soie

August 28, 1893
Rue de l'Amiscourt
Giverny

It was chilly in my garden this morning. Monsieur Seurel showed Lizzy and me how to turn pumpkins on their vines, just so. "To make them grow full and round," he said. When we went back inside, we saw steamer trunks in the front hall. The labels read:

A: Monsieur et Madame
glidden
Chez Vitse
20 rue Scheffer
Paris

Raymonde says the trunks are being sent ahead by train. I told Lizzy how Raymonde put spiders in the trunks last spring to keep moths away. At first she didn't believe me, but Raymonde told her herself, "Mais, oui!" But, of course! Everybody here puts spiders in their woolens. And, just as Raymonde promised, we didn't get one moth hole in any of our clothes!

Mama says to leave my "sabots" here. Wooden shoes are for the country. In Paris, I'll wear buttoned boots and silk shoes. Then she shook the straw out of Toby's basket and lined it with soft blue velvet instead. Only four more days until we leave for Paris: "un, deux, trois, quatre!"

For dessert tonight, we are having Raymonde's cherry "Clafoutis." Yummm.

Cherry Clafoutis
PREHEAT OVEN TO 375°

Take **4** cups of ripe cherries, pitted and stemmed, and put them in a buttered pie pan. PACK THEM TIGHTLY!

Make a batter with

3 eggs
2/3 cup sugar
1 1/4 cups whole milk
a pinch of salt
2 tsps. Vanilla extract

and beat well.
Pour batter over cherries and bake 45 minutes until puffed and golden.

Voici Le Clafoutis!

les cerises

l'araignée

la toile d'araignée

September 1, 1893
20 rue Scheffer
Paris

Finally we're in Paris! I love our big apartment. From the balcony, we can see the river Seine and, above it, the Eiffel Tower, the tallest tower in the world. I can't wait to visit that! At night the lights come on and the tower looks pink. It's the most beautiful sight I've ever seen.

Mama said she is exhausted from the trip, but I'm not a bit tired. This morning Monsieur Seurel came for us before the sun was up. It's a good thing the trunks and painting supplies went on ahead because after we picked up the Fosters and their luggage, there wasn't room in the coach for even a tube of paint! I sat on Papa's lap, with Toby on mine. Raymonde climbed up on top of the carriage to sit with Monsieur Seurel. With a team of four horses the carriage went so quickly we were at the train station in Vernon in the blink of an eye.

Monsieur Seurel settled us on the train. He promised to look after my garden. Lizzy and I waved to him out the window until the train went around a bend and we could not see him anymore. Lizzy and I played cards and ate the lunch Raymonde brought. The next thing we knew, we were in Paris!

The Gare Saint-Lazare is a very busy station. Everybody is in a hurry. I could tell Papa was glad to see Monsieur Durand-Ruel waiting for us on the platform. He brought three porters to help with our luggage! It's very noisy, too, under that big glass roof. Everywhere is the sound of wheels grinding and engines whistling and hissing clouds of blue and gray smoke. Monsieur Durand-Ruel had to shout to tell Papa about the time Monsieur Monet got permission to make paintings in the station. He put on his very best clothes and told the stationmaster he was a famous artist. Then he set up his easel right on the rails and began to paint. Not only that, he wouldn't let the trains leave the station until he was through with them!

Today, Mama and I went to market. We don't have a market like that in Boston! Fruits and vegetables are piled to the sky. And mountains of oysters smell of the sea. With some milk from the "laitière" and flowers from the "bouquetière," our baskets were filled to the top. I could tell Mama was glad I was there to help carry them.

When we got home, I found Papa in the studio. He took me by the hand and said, "Come, let's be Parisians today." We went to a café on an avenue called the Champs-Elysées. Papa says the streets of Paris were dark, narrow and twisty until Emperor Napoléon decided to make Paris the most beautiful city in the world. He hired a man named Baron Haussmann to tear down old buildings and fill the city with parks, gardens and wide avenues lined with trees. I have never seen so many people in one place. There are tables and chairs all up and down the sidewalk. And so many carriages on the avenue — sometimes as many as eight across — that you cannot see to the other side. Papa and I lifted our glasses and cried, "Vive Paris!" Long live Paris!

1   PARIS. — L'Arc de Triomphe et les Champs-Élysées. — LL.

When we walked into the courtyard of our apartment we saw someone peering at us from behind a curtain. Papa says she is the "concierge," the eyes and ears of the building. It is her business to know everything that goes on. And to bring us our mail. She is not very friendly, though. Neither is her little dog, Puce, which means "Flea." He sits on her lap and growls when he sees us. Papa says Puce is well-named because he is always scratching himself.

le poivron rouge

l'ail rose

les choux

le bouquet

The Marionette Show

September 30, 1893
20 rue Scheffer
Paris

Today, Papa took Lizzy and me to the Jardin des Tuileries, the Tuileries gardens, to paint "en plein air." It's a huge park right in the middle of Paris. While Papa set up his easel, Lizzy and I went to a tiny outdoor theater to see a marionette show.

When we got back, Papa was talking with his old friend, Mr. Maurice Prendergast. No matter where we go, Papa runs into painters from Boston! Mr. Prendergast told Papa he is in Paris to study at a painting school called the Académie Julian. Then he made a quick little oil sketch on a small wooden board. He called it a "pochade" and said everyone in Paris is doing them.

After dinner, the dressmaker came to fit us for our dresses for the exhibition. My dress is made of velvet—Prussian blue with stockings to match. Mama is wearing green silk and a hat with an ostrich feather on it.

Lizzy and Me

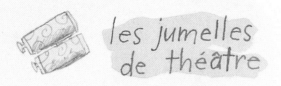

October 8, 1893
20 rue Scheffer
Paris

This morning Papa and I went to the Louvre museum. You can spend a whole day and not see half of what is there. The galleries are filled with painters making paintings of paintings. Papa said some are art students hoping to learn the ways of old masters by copying their work. Others make paintings to sell to tourists. They all have to have a permit, a piece of paper that says they are allowed to paint in the museum. He told me that when Monsieur Monet got his permit, he walked straight past the paintings of the old masters, up to a window on the second floor. Then he set his easel up on the balcony and painted the city spread out before him!

When we left the museum, it was dark and rainy. For a "sou," we rented an umbrella to cross a bridge over the river Seine. When we got to the other side, we handed it to a man waiting there. Then we saw a man selling maps of Paris and Papa bought one for me. I'm going to mark every place we visit on it.

When we got home, we found Monsieur Durand-Ruel waiting for Papa. He has already sold fifteen of Papa's paintings! To celebrate, he took us to the opera. We climbed a grand marble staircase and sat in a tiny box high above the stage. Everywhere was soft red velvet and gold. And, above our heads, a sparkly chandelier—the biggest one in the world, I bet. Papa says it weighs six tons! All at once, I thought I saw Monsieur and Madame Monet. With Mama's opera glasses, I had a closer look and saw Monsieur Monet looking right back at me! I didn't dare look again until the final curtain. By then the Monets had gone. I can't wait to tell Lizzy about this!

les
parapluies

le sorbet
à la framboise

le sorbet
à l'abricot

le sorbet
au citron

Tonight was the exhibition. After Mama and Papa said goodnight, I relit my lamp. I am far too excited to sleep. I love Paris! And exhibitions! Everybody was there, even the Perrys. Lizzy and I were so happy to see Edith. She has already been to an exhibition and knows all about them. "Follow me," she said, and then she led us through the crowd to a table with iced grenadine and yummy "sorbets," sherbets made of delicious fruits. I liked "framboise"— raspberry—the best. There was fizzy champagne and we had a sip of that, too. Then Edith pointed out Miss Cassatt, a tall woman with her back to us. She turned around and I thought I saw a fur muff on her arm. When it yawned I knew it was her dog, Batty!

Batty

As we were looking at the paintings, a pretty girl came up to talk to Edith. Her name is Julie Manet and she is fifteen. When Edith told her we live in Giverny, she said she and her mother were just there—visiting Monsieur Monet!   ⟶

GIVERNY

4

5

2

3

CHAMPS-ÉLYSÉES

12

6

7

1

20
rue
Scheffer

SEINE

8

9

10

Paris

11

N

O   E

S

After the exhibition, we all went to a restaurant called Café Riche. I hoped I would sit next to Julie Manet and I did. She likes to paint, too, and has a greyhound named Laertes.

All at once there was a quarrel. Miss Cassatt's good friend, the artist Monsieur Degas, told a painter named Monsieur Renoir that his paintings look as if they're painted with balls of wool! Monsieur Renoir turned crimson, then violet, and marched out of the restaurant. Julie says it's not at all unusual for artists to quarrel at the dinner table. But Monsieur Renoir should not have left before dessert was served! Delicious "Pêche à la Melba," Peach Melba, named for the opera singer, Nellie Melba. She must like peaches and vanilla ice cream with raspberries as much as I do.

I wonder what Mama is planning for my birthday. She won't tell me — it's a surprise.

1. Chez nous
2. Longchamp Racecourse Bois de Boulogne
3. L'Arc de Triomphe
4. Gare St. Lazare
5. The Opera
6. The Tuileries
7. Louvre Museum
8. Flower Market
9. Notre Dame
10. Eiffel Tower
11. Luxembourg Gardens
12. Fernando Circus

22. PARIS — Allée des Acacias

le chapeau en mousseline de soie

le chapeau de paille

October 31, 1893
The Longchamp Racecourse
The Bois de Boulogne
Paris

When I took Papa tea this morning, he was still working on the painting he started in the Tuileries gardens. All at once he put his paintbrush down and said, "Let's go to the horse races! Something there will inspire me."

We went by carriage (a six-seater with cushions of white satin) through the Bois de Boulogne, the biggest park in Paris. Mama wore a chiffon hat with a pink silk rose, and I, my new straw hat with crimson streamers. On the way, we saw Julie Manet and her mother with Monsieur Renoir. He was making a sketch of a woman on a dappled horse and a boy on a pony to match.

When Julie heard where we were going, she asked if she could join us. She loves the racecourse and goes to the races often—sometimes with her friend, Monsieur Degas. She says that Monsieur Degas always serves his guests the same dinner: chicken, salad and fruit preserves. Then he makes them sit for a portrait. First, he moves their arms and legs about just so—until he likes the pose. Then they have to sit perfectly still for three minutes while he takes the photograph. Julie says he never takes photographs in daylight—only by lamplight or the light of the moon.

The horses are at the starting gate—more later.

November 8, 1893
20 rue Scheffer
Paris

Never have I had such a birthday! Or such presents! A beautiful French doll from Mama, and, from Papa, a little easel of my very own. And a set of pastels—sticks of color that break easily if I'm not careful. Toby gave me a box of those chocolate mice I like so much.

Then we were off to the Cirque Fernando, the Fernando Circus. There were dancing bears and dogs in pantaloons playing the drums. I liked the tightrope walker in her sparkling costume best of all.

After, we met the Fosters at the Eiffel Tower. There is a lot more inside that tower than I ever knew! It has restaurants, a theater, even a weather station up top to measure how hard the wind blows. Not only that, Monsieur Gustave Eiffel, the man who designed the tower, built himself an apartment in it, way up high. So he can look out over Paris at night, I bet. When the gas lamps come on, they twinkle like stars all over the city. No wonder Paris is called "The City of Light!"

At dinner, I opened Lizzy's presents: a tiny Eiffel Tower and a new journal. When the waiter brought my birthday cake to the table, it had "Vive Charlotte" written right across it. Bravo, Monsieur Eiffel, for your beautiful tower and everything in it!

une belle poupée

VIVE CHARLOTTE

mon gâteau
d'anniversaire

mes
cadeaux

November 15, 1893
20 rue Scheffer
Paris

After hearing about the Académie Julian from Mr. Prendergast, Papa decided to study there, too, and today he let me go to class with him.

The classroom was hot and noisy. Crowded, too. The model posed a long time without moving a muscle. While Papa worked at his easel, I made a small drawing of her to put in the blue frame I bought at the flea market. After class, students scrape the paint off their palettes by rubbing them against the walls—I never saw that before!

Later, Mama took me to a store called Deyrolle. There were animals for sale everywhere: lions and tigers, ostriches—even a polar bear! They all looked real, but Mama said they were stuffed. She went off to find feathers while I looked at the butterfly collections. You can buy anything in Paris!

Now Mama is making a mask out of "plumes de paon," peacock feathers. Monsieur Gerome, who has the studio next to Papa's, is giving a fancy-dress party. Right there in his studio! Lizzy and I can't go. It's for grownups only. "Quel dommage!" What a shame!

"Il neige!" It's snowing!
Not a sound from below...
Paris is quiet under a blanket of snow...

les masques

November 30, 1893
20 rue Scheffer
Paris

Tonight is the fancy-dress party. Mama looked beautiful in her mask of peacock feathers with violet satin ribbons. And Papa, very dashing in a mask he painted himself. After Raymonde and I had supper, Lizzy came over to play cards. When I opened the door to let her in, Toby ran out. We chased him down the hall...into Monsieur Gerome's studio!

At first, nobody saw us—they were all too busy talking and eating. Suddenly, Toby barked at one of the guests—a monkey in a silk top hat! The monkey leapt from his little chair onto a man's head, chattering loudly. I was afraid Mama would be angry, but everybody laughed and so did she.

Monsieur Gerome said we were just in time for dessert: "Boules de Neige," snowballs made of meringue. Later, he told me the monkey, whose name is Jacques, wears the top hat when he is good. When he is bad, he is dressed like a ragamuffin. I'd like to see that, too!

le haut-de-forme

December 1, 1893
20 rue Scheffer
Paris

This afternoon, I went to Papa's studio to take him some tea. He was staring at a landscape he started in Giverny. He must have been thinking very hard. He scarcely saw me—or the tea.

I set up my easel. Onto my palette I squeezed the colors of summer. I made a painting of our garden in Giverny. Mama's roses were in bloom. The hydrangeas were puffs of blue.

Tonight is a cold, starry night. With snow piled everywhere. Papa hailed a sleigh to take us to dinner, and we glided along quiet streets. When we got to the restaurant, we were greeted by Monsieur le patron, the owner. "Ooh la la!" he said, "This is nothing like the blizzard of 1880. There was so much snow then they had to shovel it onto carts and empty it into the river Seine."

At dinner, Monsieur Durand-Ruel and Papa spoke quietly until dessert came. I could not hear what they were saying.

Les couleurs d'été

ROSE

JAUNE DE CHROME

BLEU DE COBALT

VERT

BLEU CIEL

l'hortensia   le rosier

December 2, 1893
20 rue Scheffer
Paris

At breakfast this morning, Papa put his teacup down and said that after Christmas we'd be going back to Giverny. When I asked why, he told me he is not a figure painter or a painter of city scenes. He is a landscape painter—and so Giverny, with its river valley and soft, changing light, suits him better than Paris. And, anyway, there are too many distractions in Paris, too many things to see and do. At first I was sad because we have not seen and done them all. But Mama promised we will visit again. And she told Papa that he changes his mind as often as Parisian ladies change hats. Then she took me Christmas shopping.

We got Toby a collar with a silver bell. And Raymonde, a cookbook called "Pot au Feu." She saw Monsieur Monet's cook reading it and wants a copy for herself. We found a fur hat for Papa for when he paints outdoors on cold days. And a "tablier," an apron, for Monsieur Seurel with pockets for gloves and gardening tools. I can't wait to see him again—and my garden! And for Lizzy: a travel journal bound in leather for other trips we'll take together!

Only twelve days until Christmas!

le collier de Toby

le journal

le livre de cuisine

la gargouille

Papa said we would have "réveillon," Christmas Eve dinner, in the shadow of Notre Dame. And we did! From the restaurant window we looked right up at the cathedral. The gargoyles were covered in snow but we could see their scary faces. Later, when the cathedral bells rang it was so loud we had to cover our ears.

When we got home, Raymonde had made a special Christmas dessert called "Croquembouche," which means "crunch in the mouth." It was a tower of cream puffs (crunchy on the outside and soft inside) held together by spun sugar. Lizzy and I had to stand on chairs to reach the cream puffs at the very top. Then we sat by the Christmas tree and I told Lizzy all about winter nights in Giverny. About bonfires and skating on the River Epte. And sleigh races across the frozen marsh.

Now it's time to sleep so Santa Claus can visit. I hope he knows we're spending Christmas in an apartment in Paris this year. I bet he does! "Joyeux Noël, Père Noël!" Merry Christmas, Santa Claus!

Christmas Day, 1893

Santa drank the champagne we left for him and ate the last of the cream puffs. He brought me a new pair of ice skates—I wanted some so badly! And a pair for Lizzy! We'll skate together on the Epte. The Seine, too, if it freezes over!

January 2, 1894
Rue de l'Amiscourt
Giverny

I'm so happy to be back in Giverny. This afternoon there was a knock on the door—it was Julie Manet! She and her mother are visiting the Monets. They would have gotten here sooner, but their train got stuck in the snow. They had to wait a long time to be dug out before the train could go on. Lizzy and I told Julie about the ice-skating party tonight. Then we went outside to make snow sculptures. The air was cold, but the sun felt warm on our cheeks. I made a dancing bear; Julie, a greyhound; and Lizzy, a monkey in a top hat. On the way home we passed Monsieur Monet. He was busy painting a snowy landscape and did not see us. A magpie flew into the scene and landed on the gate. Quickly, he painted her, too.

l'ours   le lévrier   le singe   la pie

As soon as it was dark, we set out for the river. Monsieur Seurel had strung paper lanterns in the trees to light the way. Everyone was there—even the Butler baby, bundled in furs. Monsieur Monet's son, the one who is always inventing things, put his skates on and held a pillowcase up high. The wind caught it and off he sailed into the night. Later, when we sat by the bonfire, he said the wind would have carried him all the way to Paris if he had let it.

I love my new skates ...
I can do figure eights!

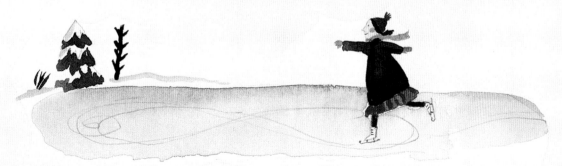

jaune de chrome

Julie came by this morning to invite me to lunch at Monsieur Monet's. She told me I had to hurry. "Vite! Vite!" she said. Quick! Quick! Lunch is served at 11:30, not a moment later.

Monsieur Monet must like chrome yellow. The whole dining room is painted that color—and everything in it, even the chairs! I was glad to see he was seated at one end of the long table and Julie and I at the other. The famous sculptor Monsieur Rodin was also there. Julie says that Monsieur Rodin fills his mouth with water when he sculpts so he can spray the clay and keep it moist and easy to work. But sometimes he misses and sprays his model, too. I don't think I would want Monsieur Rodin to make a statue of me!

We had "Canard aux Navets," duck with turnips. Monsieur Monet carved the duck himself. He must have been in a hurry to get back to his easel—he ate his lunch quickly and barely said a word. But when he left the table he took something from his pocket and handed it to me. "Pour la petite," he said. For the little one. A packet of poppy seeds! How did he know I love poppies? Julie says to find a sunny spot and scatter the seeds right over the snow. And that in the spring, up they'll pop. Is that why they're called poppies, I wonder? Wait until Lizzy hears about this... Merci, Monsieur Monet! Thank you!

No more paper... I can't wait to start my new journal and fill it with adventures.

"La Fin" The End

CREDITS

In order of journal entry

May 20, 1893
Ellen Gertrude Emmet Rand
(1875–1941)
Madame de Laisemont, 1899.
Oil on canvas, 17 ¾ x 14 ½ inches.
Collection of Rosina Rand.
Photograph by Hugh Vaughan.

June 10, 1893
Japanese Bridge in Monet's Garden,
Giverny, France.
Lilla Cabot Perry photographs, c.1889–1901.
Archives of American Art,
Smithsonian Institution.

Claude Monet (1840–1926)
Nymphéas, c.1897–1898.
Oil on canvas, 26 x 41 inches.
Los Angeles County Museum of Art,
Mrs. Fred Hathaway Bixby Bequest, M.62.8.13.
Photograph © 2004 Museum
Associates/LACMA.

June 20, 1893
Lilla Cabot Perry (1848–1933)
Self-Portrait, c.1891.
Oil on canvas, 31 ⅞ x 25 ⅝ inches.
Terra Foundation for the Arts,
Daniel J. Terra Collection, 1999.107.
Photograph courtesy of Terra Foundation
for the Arts, Chicago.

July 1, 1893
Frederick Carl Frieseke (1874–1939)
The Garden Parasol, 1910.
Oil on canvas, 57 x 76 ⅛ inches.
North Carolina Museum of Art, Raleigh.
Purchased with funds from the State of
North Carolina.

July 2, 1893
Philip Leslie Hale (1865–1931)
French Farmhouse, c. 1893.
Oil on canvas, 25 ½ x 32 inches.
Museum of Fine Arts, Boston, 1985.688.
Gift of Nancy Hale Bowers.

July 12, 1893
Mary Fairchild MacMonnies
(1858–1946)
Roses and Lilies, 1897.
Oil on canvas, 52 ⅓ x 59 ½ inches.
Musée des Beaux-Arts de Rouen.
Copyright © Giraudon/Art Resource,
New York.

September 1, 1893
Claude Monet (1840–1926)
La Gare Saint-Lazare, 1877.
Oil on canvas, 29 ¼ x 40 ¼ inches.
Musée d'Orsay, Paris. Copyright © Réunion des
Musées Nationaux/Art Resource, New York.
Photograph by Herve Lewandowski.

September 30, 1893
Maurice Brazil Prendergast (1858–1924)
The Luxembourg Garden, Paris, 1892–1894.
Oil on canvas, 12 ⅞ x 9 ⅝ inches.
Terra Foundation for the Arts, Daniel J. Terra
Collection, 1992.68. Photograph courtesy of
Terra Foundation for the Arts, Chicago.

Théâtre des Marionettes: cliché Seéberger Frères,
Arch. Photo © Centre des Monuments
Nationaux, Paris.

Jardin du Luxembourg (detail): cliché Seéberger
Frères, Arch. Photo © Centre des Monuments
Nationaux, Paris.

October 8, 1893
Charles Courtney Curran (1861–1942)
Paris at Night, 1889.
Oil on panel, 9 1/16 x 12 ¼ inches.
Terra Foundation for the Arts, Daniel J. Terra
Collection, 1989.12. Photograph courtesy of
Terra Foundation for the Arts, Chicago.

October 30, 1893
Hilaire-Germain Edgar Degas
(1834–1917)
Woman Viewed from Behind, c.1879.
Oil on canvas, 32 x 29 ¾ inches.
National Gallery of Art, collection of
Mr. and Mrs. Paul Mellon. Photograph
© 2002 Board of Trustees, National Gallery of
Art, Washington, D.C.

October 31, 1893
Pierre-Auguste Renoir (1841–1919)
Riding in the Bois de Boulogne, 1873.
Oil on canvas, 102 ¼ x 89 inches.
Hamburg Kunsthalle, Hamburg, Germany,
HKH149517. Photograph courtesy of the
Bridgeman Art Library.

November 8, 1893
Georges Garen (unknown)
Illumination of the Eiffel Tower at the 1889
Exposition, 1889.
Color lithograph, 12 x 19 inches.
Collection Dennis Cate and Lynn Gumpert,
New York.

November 30, 1893
Gustave Caillebotte (1848–1894)
View of Rooftops (Snow), c. 1878.
Oil on canvas, 25 ¼ x 32 ¼ inches.
Musée d'Orsay, Paris. Copyright © Réunion des
Musées Nationaux/Art Resource, New York.

January 2, 1894
Claude Monet (1840–1926)
The Magpie, 1869.
Oil on canvas, 35 x 51 inches.
Musée d'Orsay, Paris. Copyright © Réunion des
Musées Nationaux/Art Resource, New York.

"The Artists" section
Mary Cassatt (1844–1926)
In the Omnibus, 1890–1891.
Drypoint and aquatint in color plate,
14 7/16 x 10 9/16 inches.
Terra Foundation for the Arts, Daniel J. Terra
Collection, 1999.27. Photograph courtesy of
Terra Foundation for the Arts, Chicago.

All other photographs and ephemera
collection of the author.

THE ARTISTS

GUSTAVE CAILLEBOTTE (1848–1894) A Parisian by birth, Gustave Caillebotte often painted street scenes of Baron Haussmann's newly designed Paris. A naval engineer as well as an artist, he enjoyed sailing a yacht that he built himself from Paris to Giverny to visit his good friend, Claude Monet. Caillebotte became an important collector and supporter of his fellow Impressionist painters.

CHARLES COURTNEY CURRAN (1861–1942) Curran was born in Hartford, Kentucky, but spent most of his childhood in Sandusky, Ohio. As a young man, he studied at the National Academy of Design and the Art Students League in New York. In 1888 he enrolled at the Académie Julian in Paris. Inspired one rainy night by the shimmering reflections of Paris's newly installed gas lamps, he set out to paint *Paris at Night*.

HILAIRE-GERMAIN EDGAR DEGAS (1834–1917) The son of a wealthy Italian banker who settled in Paris, Degas studied at the Ecole des Beaux-Arts. He was not inspired by nature as were most of his fellow Impressionists, but rather by the ballet, horse racing and portraiture. He developed a keen interest in the new art of photography, and used the camera to make studies for his paintings. As he grew older, his eyesight deteriorated and he turned to sculpture.

FREDERICK CARL FRIESEKE (1874–1939) Originally from Michigan, Frieseke first visited Giverny in 1900 and settled there in 1906 with his new bride, Sadie. They rented a small cottage with a beautiful sunlit garden filled with flowers and surrounded by high walls. It was here, on golden afternoons, that Frieseke created many of the color-saturated figure paintings for which he is famous.

ELLEN DAY HALE (1855–1940) Hale was born in Worcester, Massachusetts. In 1882, she traveled to Paris to study at the Académie Julian. While there, she wrote articles on the Parisian art scene for the *Boston Traveler*. From time to time she traveled to Giverny to join her brother, Philip Leslie Hale, painting *en plein air*.

PHILIP LESLIE HALE (1865–1931) Philip Leslie Hale, a portrait and landscape painter from Boston, traveled to Paris in 1887 and enrolled at the the Ecole des Beaux-Arts as well as the Académie Julian. He spent his summers in Giverny, often in the company of his sister, Ellen Day Hale. In late 1892, Hale returned to Boston where he was involved with the Impressionist movement not only as a painter but also as an art teacher and as a writer and critic for the *Boston Herald*.

MARY FAIRCHILD MACMONNIES LOW (1858–1946) Born in New Haven, Connecticut, Mary Fairchild studied first at the St. Louis School of Fine Art, then at the Académie Julian in Paris. In 1888 she married the American sculptor Frederick MacMonnies. They lived in Paris and summered in Giverny until 1898 when they moved to Giverny permanently. Their next-door neighbor was Isadora Duncan, a famous American dancer, who liked to dance in her garden.

CLAUDE MONET (1840–1926) Oscar Claude Monet was born in Paris but moved to Le Havre with his family when he was five. Even as a boy, he was gifted and encouraged by his parents and teachers to study art. In 1859, he returned to Paris to study art at Académie Suisse. In 1862, he met Pierre-Auguste Renoir and Alfred Sisley, and together they founded an independent group of artists. They organized their first group exhibition in 1874. Monet's painting *Impression: Sunrise* gave rise to the name "Impressionism" and defined the group's style. In 1883, after his first wife, Camille, died, Monet moved with Alice Hoschedé and her six children to Giverny. They settled into the Maison du Pressoir, or "Cider-Press House," where he lived—painting, gardening and landscaping—for the next forty-three years.

LILLA CABOT PERRY (1848–1933) Boston-born Lilla Cabot Perry spent ten summers in Giverny with her family, staying often in a farmhouse with a garden adjoining that of Monet, her mentor. Perry painted landscapes as well as figures, often children. She bought paintings directly from Monet's studio and promoted his work as well as that of American Impressionist painters.

MAURICE BRAZIL PRENDERGAST (1858–1924) Maurice Prendergast was born in St. John's, Newfoundland, where his father had a trading post. At the age of ten, he moved with his family to Boston, Massachusetts. In 1891, he and his brother Charles, a frame maker, had saved enough money to travel to Paris. There, he enrolled at the academies Julian and Colarossi and was inspired to paint many scenes of Parisians enjoying their beautiful parks and gardens.

ELLEN GERTRUDE EMMET RAND (1875–1941) Born in San Francisco, Rand first studied painting with William Merritt Chase at the Shinnecock Summer School of Art on Long Island, New York, and then with Frederick MacMonnies in Paris and in Giverny. On a trip to England, she met John Singer Sargent, whose work she greatly admired. In 1900, after her European travels, Rand settled in New York City where she had a highly successful career as a portraitist.

PIERRE-AUGUSTE RENOIR (1841–1919) The son of a tailor and a dressmaker, Renoir was apprenticed to a porcelain painter before he enrolled at Gleyre's studio, where he studied with Claude Monet and Alfred Sisley. He later attended the Ecole des Beaux-Arts. A versatile artist, he painted dancers and dance halls, portraits of society ladies, circus acts, still lifes and nudes. Like Degas, he turned to sculpture later in life, as his eyesight began to fail.

AUGUSTE RODIN (1840–1917) Rodin, a close friend of Monet's and a frequent guest at his table in Giverny, devoted himself to drawing by the time he was ten years old. At fifteen, as an art student at the Petite Ecole, he discovered clay and showed promise as a sculptor. At eighteen, to help support his family, he went to work sculpting decorative stonework for the city of Paris. He traveled to Italy in 1875 where he studied the works of Michelangelo. When he was seventy-six Rodin turned his sculptures, along with his personal art collection, over to the French government. These can be seen at the Musée Rodin in Paris and are still placed just as Rodin set them.

MARY CASSATT (1844–1926)

Born in Pittsburgh, Pennsylvania, to wealthy parents, Mary Cassatt traveled to Paris when she was twenty-two to study painting and applied for a permit to copy works of art at the Louvre. She became a close friend of Edgar Degas and helped the Impressionists by promoting their work in the United States. Inspired by an exhibition of Japanese woodcuts at the Ecole des Beaux-Arts in 1890, Mary Cassatt became an accomplished printmaker as well as painter. The color print *In the Omnibus* shows women traveling independently by public transportation, a new and important aspect of life for modern women. Mary Cassatt was the only American ever to be invited to exhibit with the French Impressionists.

AUTHOR'S NOTE

Charlotte Glidden is not a real person, although there could very well have been an American girl just like her in Paris in the early 1890s. Her journal is, however, based on historical fact. American painters, inspired by the works of French artists such as Claude Monet, Edgar

Degas and Auguste Renoir, flocked to Paris, the art capital of the world to study at the academies, visit the museums and view exhibitions of the work of the French masters. Some, like Mary Cassatt and the fictitious Glidden family of this book, rented apartments and studios and stayed on to paint outdoors—*en plein air*—in the French Impressionist style. Like Parisians, they frequented cafés on the grand boulevards, strolled in the city's beautiful parks and gardens, and attended the opera, the ballet and the horse races in the Bois de Boulogne. With the new French railway system, they could easily travel back and forth from the heart of Paris to artist colonies in the countryside such as Giverny.

I would like to give special thanks to the Terra Foundation for the Arts, Chicago, and the Centre des Monuments Nationaux, Paris, and to acknowledge the diary of Julie Manet. The only child of the painter Berthe Morisot and Eugene Manet (the younger brother of Edouard Manet) and a painter herself, Julie Manet grew up among the Impressionists and the diary she kept as a teenager was a source of inspiration for this book.

Joan M. Knight